DATE DUE

MAR 1 2 2008			
APR 0 2 2008		NOV 0 7 2014	
SEP 2 4 2008			
OCT 1 6 2008			
NOV 1 0 2008			
JAN 2 7 2009			
MAR 0 4 2009			
MAR 3 1 2009			
SEP 1 6 2009			
FEB 0 4 2010			
SEP 2 1 2010			
JAN 0 2 2014			
OCT 0 5 2018			
OCT 0 5 2018			

THE FISH GUT EXPERIMENT

by R. Starke

illustrated by Tom Jellett
Cover illustration by Chip Boles

Librarian Reviewer
Marci Peschke
Librarian, Dallas Independent School District
MA Education Reading Specialist, Stephen F. Austin State University
Learning Resources Endorsement, Texas Women's University

Reading Consultant
Elizabeth Stedem
Educator/Consultant, Colorado Springs, CO
MA in Elementary Education, University of Denver, CO

STONE ARCH BOOKS
Minneapolis   San Diego

First published in the United States in 2008
by Stone Arch Books
151 Good Counsel Drive, P.O. Box 669
Mankato, Minnesota 56002
www.stonearchbooks.com

First published in Australia in 1997 by Lothian Books
(now Hachette Livre Australia Pty Ltd)

Published in arrangement with Hachette Livre Australia.

Library of Congress Cataloging-in-Publication Data
Starks, R.

The Fish Gut Experiment / by R. Starks; illustrated by Tom
Jellett.

p. cm. — (Shade Books)

Summary: While researching aging for a class project, Jenna
becomes obsessed with staying young and, after reading part of
an Aldous Huxley book about a man on a similar quest, tries
an experiment on her parents without knowing the possible side
effects.

ISBN-13: 978-1-59889-862-0 (library binding)

ISBN-10: 1-59889-862-0 (library binding)

ISBN-13: 978-1-59889-918-4 (paperback)

ISBN-10: 1-59889-918-X (paperback)

[1. Aging—Fiction. 2. Family life—Fiction. 3. Food—
Experiments—Fiction. 4. Horror stories.] I. Jellett, Tom, ill.
II. Title.
PZ7.S79558Fis 2008
[Fic]—dc22   2007003738

Art Director: Heather Kindseth
Graphic Designer: Kay Fraser

1 2 3 4 5 6 12 11 10 09 08 07

Printed in the United States of America

TABLE OF CONTENTS

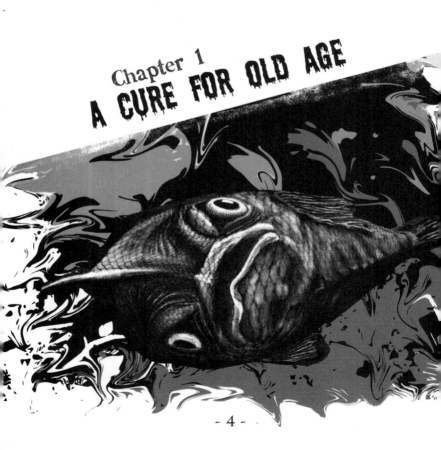

Chapter 1
A CURE FOR OLD AGE

It was the scariest picture that Jenna had ever seen.

Everybody in it was smiling. No one seemed to know what lay ahead for them. That just made it scarier.

Jenna handed the photo back to her mother. Jenna's face showed her feelings.

"What?" her mom asked. She moved the baby from her shoulder to her hip.

"Everybody looks so old," Jenna said.

"They do not!" her mom said.

"They do. Take another look at the older photo. The difference is really scary."

Jenna pointed at the old black-and-white photograph on the fridge door.

"Jenna, that school photo was taken twenty-five years ago. This one was taken last week! People don't stay young forever, you know," Mom said.

"That's for sure," Jenna said.

"You wait. You'll be older yourself one day." Her mother stuck the new photograph on the fridge. Then she marched out of the kitchen.

Jenna sighed.

Ever since she started her school project on aging, she had learned that old people were very touchy about their age.

You couldn't stop someone on the street and ask, "What does it feel like to be old?"

Nine times out of ten, they'd look really mad. They would say that they couldn't answer the question because they didn't think of themselves as old.

Jenna had realized that most adults did not want to admit that their best years were over. That included her mom.

Even her dad, who thought almost everything was funny, didn't laugh at jokes about baldness anymore. Now his own head looked like a smooth, shiny egg.

Jenna found her father in the old class photograph.

He had a bright young face and messy hair that flopped over his right eye. He didn't wear glasses back then. There weren't any bags under his eyes, and he didn't have a double chin.

Then there was Jenna's mother. She was a thin girl with a pretty smile and a bright face. She looked exactly like Jenna. That, Jenna thought, was the scariest part.

Her eyes flipped back and forth between the two photos. At what age did you start to get old? When you were twenty-one? Thirty?

Jenna tried to imagine being old. She'd probably look a lot like her mom, who was thirty-nine. Mom wasn't young. That meant that she was old.

Jenna shivered. She looked down at the backs of her hands. She imagined them wrinkled and covered with brown spots.

Maybe in the next few years or so, science would find a cure for old age and save her.

Jenna removed the two photographs from the door of the fridge and put them into her project folder.

She could use them for a before-and-after illustration.

Then she began to peel the vegetables for dinner.

Chapter 2
INSIDES AND OUTSIDES

At the table that evening, her mother noticed that the photographs were gone.

"Jenna thinks that photo of our class reunion is too gross to show anyone," Mom said. "She thinks we're all a bunch of old people."

"Well, honey, we are," said Jenna's father. He shoveled mashed potatoes and gravy into his mouth. "We aren't exactly young, you know."

"I took the pictures down so I can use them in my project," Jenna said.

Her mother looked at her. "What project?" she asked.

"For social studies," Jenna replied. "We're studying old age."

"Well, thanks very much! You can just put them right back on the fridge. I'm not being anyone's example of old age!" Jenna's mom said.

"Oh, let her have them," Dad said, scraping his plate. "I was going to take them down anyway. Who wants to be reminded of one's lost childhood all of the time?"

"Do you mean me?" Mom asked angrily.

"I mean both of us," Dad explained. "You can't expect to look the same at forty as you did when you were fourteen."

"Really? Such wisdom," Mom said in a sour voice. "Well, I'm not forty yet."

Mom got up from the table and looked at Jenna. "You know, the outside might look different, but the inside is exactly the same." Then she stomped out of the room.

Dad made a face at Jenna. "She's just moody. It's hard work, having a new baby. Take her a cup of tea when you're done clearing the table," he said.

But baby James has been here for three months, Jenna thought. And Mom wasn't like this until recently.

In fact, when James was born, Mom had been excited. "We've been waiting for you for ten years, my darling," Jenna had overheard her mom saying to the baby.

She thought about what her mother had said, about a person's outside being different but the inside being the same.

Could that be true?

Wouldn't the insides change, too, over the years?

Even if the inside did stay the same, wasn't the outside package important, too? If a can was dented in a store, the store would sell it at half price.

Jenna made a mug of tea and took it into her mother's room. Mom was lying stretched out on the bed. Her face was green.

"You look gross," Jenna said. She put the mug down on the bedside table.

"It's a seaweed and mud mask," Mom said. "Don't make me talk, it'll crack."

"What does it do?" Jenna asked.

Mom handed her a tube.

Jenna read the tube's label, "Rich mud gives skin a beautiful glow and energy."

She wondered if there was anything you could take that would give your insides a beautiful glow and energy. Jenna didn't think putting mud on your face would help you stay young.

Jenna suddenly remembered a TV show she'd once seen. It was about a girl who had a disease that made her body age really fast.

She was only seven, but the little girl had looked like a wrinkly apple doll, or one of the witches in a fairy tale.

It was enough to give you nightmares.

Chapter 3
JENNA'S NIGHTMARE

As the moon slipped behind the clouds, a thick, wet fog suddenly appeared.

It clouded the tops of the trees and hung from the branches.

Jenna hurried through the forest. She couldn't see the ground under her feet or the sky above.

She was too scared to stop.

Someone, or something, was chasing her. She had seen a dark shadow.

Whatever it was, it was there in the darkness behind her. It was out to get her.

Her heart was thumping, and the ticking of her watch was loud.

She was afraid that either noise might give her away.

She ripped her watch from her wrist and flung it away into the bushes. It rolled along behind her, ticking.

Her eyes strained to see in the darkness.

Jenna stumbled through the gloom.

A branch slapped her face. Thorns tore at her skin.

Strength seemed to be leaking out of her.

Her legs felt like they couldn't move any faster than a slow shuffle.

Jenna gasped for breath as she pushed through the forest.

Shadowy branches reached out and grabbed her clothing.

It seemed like the branches were trying to keep her from moving.

All the time, the thing chased her.

At last, Jenna could go no farther. There was a pain in her chest and a throbbing in her side.

Her throat felt dry and parched, and her lips were cracked.

She sank to her knees, waiting in fear for whatever horrible fate would happen.

The watch rolled up to her and came to rest at her side.

It was no longer chasing her. It was only her same old watch.

"I wonder how long I've been running," Jenna said.

She picked up the watch.

For the first time, Jenna noticed that her hands were shrunken and shaped like claws.

She stared at them in horror. When had that happened?

She looked at her watch. Was that really the time? It couldn't possibly be that late.

Heavy footsteps behind her suddenly made the ground shake.

Jenna's blood froze.

Not daring to turn around, hardly daring to breathe, she kept her head down.

She felt something behind her. The sky grew dark, as if huge wings were hanging over her.

There was an evil laugh.

Then something powerful grabbed her hair and ripped every strand right out of her head.

Jenna looked down. The hair was all around her, like long gray strings from an old mop.

She opened her mouth to scream. Every tooth in her head fell out. They plopped onto the ground between her bony knees.

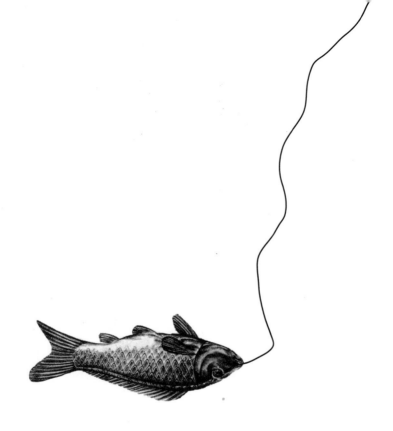

Chapter 4
ENDINGS

The nightmare stayed in Jenna's mind all week. She started to feel worried when she looked at people, especially old people.

She watched bent old people moving slowly along the street, carrying home their groceries in plastic bags.

They were usually alone. Jenna noticed that even couples hardly talked or laughed together, like she and her friends did.

In the pictures she clipped from magazines, the old men were toothless and bald. The old women had hairs on their chins and skinny necks.

Grumpy old men. Crabby old women.

Jenna started to think a lot about endings.

That was partly because of her project. It was also partly because it was late autumn.

Endings were all around her, everywhere she looked.

Dry leaves covered the sidewalk she walked on to school in the morning.

At home, the leaves clogged the gutters and piled up along the driveway.

Jenna couldn't look around without seeing some kind of death.

The bare branches of trees were stripped of their summer richness. They showed ugly power lines, crumbling chimneys, and old peeling paint.

* * *

Standing in front of the bathroom mirror each morning, Jenna would check her face for signs of aging.

She looked at the skin beneath her jaw and at her upper arms. Jenna knew it was only a matter of time.

As she brushed her teeth she wondered if they would always be hers. Would they stay with her all her life? Or would they drop into the ground before she did, the way they had in her dream?

Old age didn't just make you look bad, Jenna thought. It was actually deadly. Lots of healthy people didn't die because they were sick. They died of old age. Jenna's own grandfather, for instance, had died in his sleep at the age of eighty-two.

He had been healthy.

That's what the doctor had said, anyway. Was that supposed to be comforting? It just about scared Jenna to death.

Science could send people to the moon and get rid of smallpox. Why couldn't it find a cure for old age?

It didn't seem like a very hard task. In fact, Jenna thought, it might be something she should investigate as part of her project.

Chapter 5
A POSSIBILITY

If Jenna had ever wondered what the worst fate in the world was, she found the answer in her local library.

The worst fate was old age.

Everything she read about it seemed to prove that old age was worse than disease or even being disabled.

Everyone got old. It didn't matter if they were rich or poor, ugly or beautiful, healthy or sick.

There had been lots of research on aging. There was even a name for the study of old age: gerontology.

Jenna spent an entire afternoon looking through books.

It was not much fun.

"Throughout the world, old women are the poorest of the poor," she read.

Poor Mom! No wonder she was worried.

"People who retire at fifty can expect another twenty years of active life," said the next book.

That didn't seem to promise much. Poor Dad. He loved tennis. He didn't have many games left.

The worst things in the books were the illustrations.

The people in them looked sad or lonely. Almost everyone wore glasses. Everyone had gray hair and wrinkles. They napped in rocking chairs with cats asleep at their feet, or lay in bed.

If they could stand they used walking sticks, or the helping hand of some kind younger person.

The only good news Jenna found was a story about a Russian farmer who was 122 years old.

There was a picture of the man in front of a log cabin. He had several great-great-grandchildren around him. He looked healthy for someone who had lived for more than a century.

Jenna read the story carefully.

She wanted to know if there were any hints about living to such an old age.

It seemed like his secret was hard work, plenty of fresh air, and eating lots of vegetables. He also tried to avoid worrying.

It didn't sound much like living to Jenna.

She went to the front desk and asked the head librarian, Miss Dodwell, for a book on the subject.

"On death and dying?" Miss Dodwell looked at her curiously.

"Well, on not dying, actually," Jenna said. She wondered if Miss Dodwell had ever read about the subject.

The librarian had gray hair that was pure white at the sides. Her face was wrinkled. Two lines went from each side of her nose down past the corners of her mouth.

"A book about not dying?" Miss Dodwell asked.

"Yes, a book about staying young and living long. A serious book by a real author," Jenna said.

Miss Dodwell thought for a moment. Then she said, "I think I have the very book you're looking for."

She typed on her computer. Jenna noticed how the skin below the woman's chin hung in a fold all the way down her neck. She wondered how the library could have such an old worker.

Then she remembered that the Russian farmer was still working in the fields.

"Yes, the book is in," said Miss Dodwell. "I'll get it for you."

She returned in a few minutes. Then she took Jenna's library card and whizzed the details through the computer.

Then she handed the book to Jenna.

The book had a plain blue cover. It looked really boring.

"*After Many a Summer,*" Jenna read aloud. "By Aldous Huxley." She'd never heard of the book or its author.

"He is a very famous writer," Miss Dodwell said.

Chapter 6
AFTER MANY A SUMMER

Jenna started reading the book that night. It was about an old millionaire who lived with his girlfriend in a castle in the California desert.

The millionaire was afraid of death. So he was paying a scientist to discover the secret of eternal life.

Also in the castle was a professor. The professor was reading through some dusty old diaries written by a British duke two hundred years earlier.

Some of it was funny. It was also one of the most frustrating books Jenna had ever read.

Every time the story got interesting, a boring character called Propter appeared. Then he talked about art and science for pages and pages.

Jenna skipped over that. Obviously the scientist was going to discover the secret of eternal life. Jenna could hardly wait to find out what it was.

* * *

It was early the next morning, as she was reading the book over her cornflakes, that Jenna realized that she was wrong.

The scientist didn't discover the secret.

The professor did, in one of the old diaries. He read that the duke had noticed that the carp in his fish pond lived for a very long time. The duke wrote about it in his diary.

He had made his own life longer by eating their chopped raw guts.

Jenna put the book down.

Raw fish guts? That was what you had to eat in order to live forever?

Well, almost forever. A few hundred years, anyway.

Jenna ate her cornflakes and thought about it.

It seemed like it would be worth it, especially since she wouldn't be the one doing the eating.

Jenna would try the carp guts on her parents first, since they needed the help.

Jenna could afford to wait a few years. Besides, it would be more scientific to see what happened to her parents first.

She went on reading. After a few pages, she came to another one of those boring speeches. She put the book down.

"What's that you're reading?" her father asked. He dipped his toast into his egg and stirred the yolk.

"Just a book. Dad, do we have any carp around here?" Jenna asked.

"Yes," Dad said. "Why?"

"School project," Jenna said.

She looked up "carp" in the dictionary. The definition read, "A large freshwater fish, *Cyprinus carpio*, known for its long life."

Jenna smiled. So it was true.

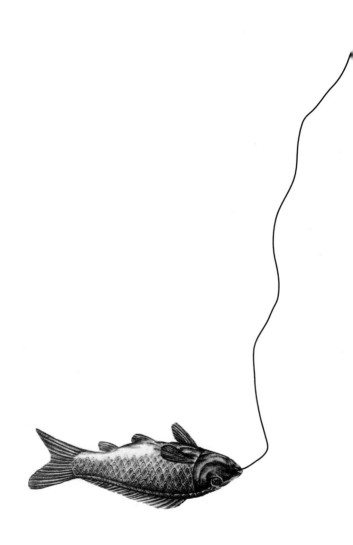

Chapter 7
THE SECRET INGREDIENT

It was harder to buy carp than Jenna expected. The fish store in town had plenty of fish like sea bass and salmon, but there was no carp.

"Not many people like it," the fish man said. "I can order it for you, though. Thursday sound okay?"

Jenna nodded. "Whole carp," she said. "With everything still inside."

"Uncleaned carp?" the man asked. He looked shocked. "Are you sure?"

"Yes," Jenna said.

"How many?" he asked.

Jenna thought about it. The duke in the story wrote in his diary that he ate ten ounces of chopped guts each day. "How much does a carp cost?" she asked.

The man shrugged. "Not much. No one eats them these days. A dollar, or a dollar fifty, maybe."

"I'll take three," Jenna said.

* * *

It was the second most disgusting thing Jenna had ever done in her life, after changing James's diaper.

Thank goodness for her mom's food processor.

Jenna ground up the carp guts in the food processor. Finally, it was just something that looked like pudding.

Jenna tasted a tiny speck on the tip of her finger and made a face.

Luckily, they were having soup for dinner. She would stir the guts into the soup. Then she would put a bunch of cheese on top.

Her parents would never notice the extra ingredient she slipped into their steaming bowls.

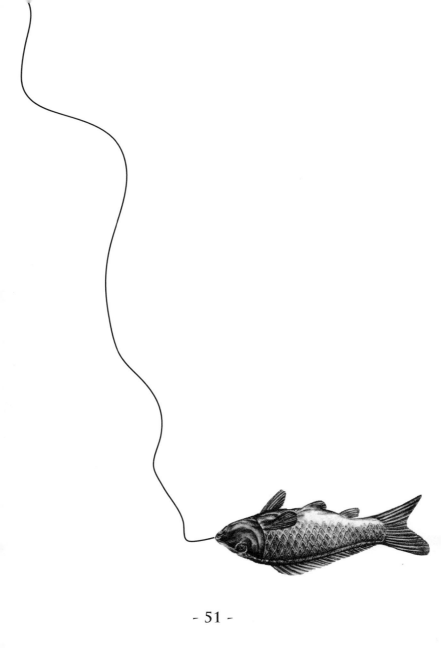

Chapter 8
NEW ENERGY

Two weeks and fourteen carp later, Jenna was almost ready to give up on the experiment.

She was sick of bringing fish home in her backpack.

She was sick of being up to her elbows in fish guts.

She was sick of trying to hide the fishy bodies in the garbage.

It did seem to be working, though. Jenna's mom and dad were healthier than ever. But Jenna was tired. There had to be an easier way.

* * *

"What do you do with all this carp?" the fish store man asked her the next Thursday. "Do you make soup or something?" the man went on.

Jenna shook her head.

"We only eat the insides. They're very healthy," she told him.

"So why not buy fish vitamin pills?" the man asked. "They'd be easier to use."

"It has to be fresh carp," Jenna said. "The raw guts are full of special bacteria."

The man shook his head. "That's a huge waste. Why don't you just buy the guts?"

Jenna stared at him. "I could do that?" she asked.

"Why not?" the fish man said. "They just get thrown away."

He made a note on a piece of paper. "Come in next week, and I'll have a bag for you," he said.

* * *

Jenna was thrilled. So much time was saved. She started adding the guts to everything. She made pudding, using twice as much chocolate to hide the fishy flavor.

"Jenna, this is so yummy!" her parents said. They ate the whole batch in a night.

Jenna made notes in her notebook. Then she made another large bowl of pudding.

The results were amazing. Dad increased his tennis games to five each week. He started jogging, too.

Mom joined a gym. "I feel so full of energy!" she sang.

Both of them glowed with health.

* * *

"Hey, come and look at this!" Dad called from the bathroom one Sunday morning.

When Jenna rushed in, he lowered his head.

"Check this out!" Dad said.

His smooth, bald head was covered with a light brown fuzz.

"It's growing back!" he cried.

Jenna had never seen him so happy. She went back to the kitchen and stirred another spoonful of the magic ingredient into the spaghetti sauce she was cooking.

It couldn't hurt.

Chapter 9
THINGS GET HAIRY

Hair was growing everywhere.

All over Jenna's mom, to be exact.

"I don't understand it," Mom said at dinner one night. "It's sort of strange, isn't it? Both of us getting hairier?"

"Coincidence," Dad said.

"Maybe it's something in the water," Mom said.

"If it was," Dad pointed out, "the whole city would be growing more hair."

"Then it must be something we ate," Mom said.

"In which case Jenna would be getting hairier, too," Jenna's dad said.

Jenna stood up and started clearing the table. "I have homework to do," she said. She escaped to the kitchen.

"Honey, you embarrassed her," she heard her mother say.

"Look, there's nothing wrong. We're just growing more hair. Getting ready for winter, or something," Dad said. "You look great, and you feel fine, don't you?"

"Better than I've felt in years," Mom said.

"So do I. So what's the problem? Who cares about a little hair?" Dad said.

Jenna was glad the subject had moved away from food.

Chapter 10
A TWIST IN THE TALE

After school the next day, Jenna took the Aldous Huxley book back to the library.

Miss Dodwell was at the front desk. "Did you enjoy it?" she asked.

"It was exactly what I was looking for," Jenna said. "Has he written any other books lately?"

"Aldous Huxley died in 1963," Miss Dodwell said.

Jenna looked at the librarian in surprise. "He did? How old was he?"

"I think he was in his late sixties," Miss Dodwell replied.

"That's not very old," Jenna said, thinking of her grandfather.

"No," Miss Dodwell agreed. "But he ate some strange things in his later years."

"Why didn't he eat chopped carp?" Jenna asked. "You know, like he wrote about in his book. It kept that old guy alive for about two hundred years."

Miss Dodwell laughed, as if Jenna had said something funny. "Well, I guess he didn't want to end up like the duke," she said with a smile. "After all, who wants to turn into an ape?"

The blood seemed to freeze in Jenna's veins. "An ape?" she asked.

"You remember how the story ends, don't you?" Miss Dodwell asked.

Jenna snatched the book from the counter. "I think I left something in here," she muttered.

She found a chair. Then, with shaking fingers, she turned to the last chapters of the book.

Why on earth hadn't she read the whole thing? She should have known there would have been a twist in the tale.

And there certainly was. A horrible, disgusting twist.

Eating chopped guts made you live a very long time. But it also made you very, very hairy.

The duke had turned into an ape-man. It was a funny ending for a book, but no laughing matter in real life.

Jenna shut the book and forced herself to think calmly.

Mom and Dad had only been eating the stuff for a few weeks, not years, like the duke had.

The hair growth might be an early sign, but there wasn't any danger that Jenna's parents would turn into apes.

Was there?

Jenna took a deep breath.

Just stop now, she told herself. Then everything will be fine. No one will ever find out.

Thank goodness she hadn't eaten any!

She decided to go home and pour the stuff down the kitchen sink. She would have to get used to the idea of getting old.

Jenna put the book on the front desk on her way out.

Miss Dodwell smiled at her. She waved a book in the air. "I found another Huxley book for you," she said. "It's about life hundreds of years in the future."

"No thank you," said Jenna. "I think I've read enough for now."

Chapter 11
LITTLE MONKEY

It was dark when Jenna got home, even though it was not yet six o'clock.

The days were getting shorter, Jenna realized.

It would be winter soon.

She let herself into the house. Her mother was singing softly in James's room.

"Jenna, is that you? Where have you been?" her mother called.

"At the library," Jenna replied. "I was working on my project."

"Come give the baby a kiss. I just fed him. You never see him these days, or play with him anymore!" her mom said.

What was the point? Jenna wondered.

James never did anything but lie in his crib or in his mom's arms. Play with him? She'd rather have a puppy.

But she pushed open the door and went into James's room.

Her mom held the baby toward Jenna. "Hold him for a minute, okay, darling?"

Jenna took the baby carefully. He was wearing a blue outfit.

There seemed to be something different about him.

His skin seemed darker. Or was it just a trick of the light?

His silky hair was getting longer and thicker. It would have to be cut soon.

The baby wiggled in her arms.

That wasn't like him.

"His eyes are brown," Jenna said in surprise. "Like little, dark, shiny buttons. I thought he had blue eyes."

"All babies have blue eyes when they're born," her mother replied.

But did all babies have that hard ridge of bone above their eyes?

Jenna looked closer.

A strong little hand reached out and grabbed her hair.

"Ouch!" she exclaimed.

She pulled back, but James's other hand shot out and grabbed more hair.

The baby opened his mouth. It was like he was grinning at Jenna.

What long arms he had, Jenna thought. And skinny little fingers, almost like claws.

She tried to pull them from her hair.

Then the truth hit her.

She stood still. Her mind spun.

The carp bacteria had come from their mom, of course. She must have given James a few bites of the pudding.

Even a small dose would have a huge effect on such a small baby.

The baby wiggled again and tugged at her hair. Jenna stared down at him in growing horror.

Mom turned around and held out her arms. "Give the little monkey to me," she said fondly.

ABOUT THE AUTHOR

Ruth Starke has worked in public relations and travel marketing, and at many other jobs. Her most interesting ones, she says, were selling French perfume, cooking on the radio, taking tourists to Kashmir, and interviewing racecar drivers. She turned to fiction writing in 1992, and since then has written over a dozen novels for young people. Ruth lives in Adelaide, Australia, where she is an English and creative writing teacher.

ABOUT THE ILLUSTRATOR

Tom Jellett has been illustrating books since graduating from the University of South Australia in 1995. He has illustrated a number of picture books and novels. Tom lives in Sydney, Australia, and works as an illustrator for *The Australian*. His work also appears regularly in *The School Magazine*.

GLOSSARY

bacteria (bak-TEER-ee-uh)—microscopic living things that exist all around, including inside the bodies of animals

century (SEN-chuh-ree)—a period of 100 years

coincidence (koh-IN-si-duhnss)—an event that happens by chance

duke (DOOK)—a member of a wealthy or high-ranking family. In England and France, some dukes ruled over parts of the country.

eternal (ee-TUR-nuhl)—lasting forever

frustrating (FRUHSS-tray-ting)—difficult or challenging

gerontology (jer-un-TOL-uh-jee)—the science of old age

ingredient (in-GREE-dee-uhnt)—one of the items used to make something

investigate (in-VESS-tuh-gate)—to find out as much as possible about something

retire (ri-TIRE)—to stop working

smallpox (SMALL-pocks)—a disease that used to be deadly, but has now been wiped out

DISCUSSION QUESTIONS

1. What are some of your feelings about getting older? What are you looking forward to? What are you not looking forward to?

2. What are the pros and cons of living forever? What would be good about it? What would be bad about it?

3. Why does Jenna try the secret ingredient on her parents? Why doesn't she try using it herself first?

4. What did Jenna's nightmare mean?

WRITING PROMPTS

1. If you could live forever (without turning into an ape-person) what would you do? Where would you live? Would you tell people how old you were? Make a list of things you would do.

2. At the end of this book, Jenna realizes that her little brother has eaten some of the carp and may turn into an ape-baby. What do you think happens next? Write a new chapter that begins where this book ends.

3. One morning, you wake up, look in the mirror, and realize that you are 100 years old! What happened? What do you do next? How do you feel about it? Write it all down!

TAKE A DEEP
BREATH AND

Janet never had a friend before Lola came along.
When Lola asks her to sleep over, Janet jumps at the
chance. She takes the bus to the Half Moon Bridge,
where Lola promised to meet her. Lola doesn't show
up . . . but a strange dog does.

STEP INTO THE SHADE!

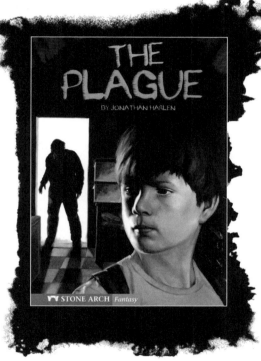

Melissa and Will just wanted to go into the pet store and take a quick look at the exotic pets. Without warning, the store's sick owner, Mr. Brinkley, bites Will on his arm! Hours later, Will becomes sick too. Do the animals carry a dangerous plague?

INTERNET SITES

Do you want to know more about subjects related to this book? Or are you interested in learning about other topics? Then check out FactHound, a fun, easy way to find Internet sites.

Our investigative staff has already sniffed out great sites for you!

Here's how to use FactHound:

1. Visit *www.facthound.com*

2. Select your grade level.

3. To learn more about subjects related to this book, type in the book's ISBN number: **1598898620**.

4. Click the **Fetch It** button.

FactHound will fetch the best Internet sites for you!